W9-BCS-599

THE NEW KING

Doreen Rappaport

pictures by E. B. Lewis

Dial Books for Young Readers New York

Published by Dial Books for Young Readers
A Division of Penguin Books USA Inc.
375 Hudson Street
New York, New York 10014

Typography by Amelia Lau Carling
Printed in Hong Kong
First Edition
1 3 5 7 9 10 8 6 4 2

Library of Congress Cataloging in Publication Data
Rappaport, Doreen.
The new king | Doreen Rappaport ;
pictures by E. B. Lewis. — 1st ed. p. cm.
Summary: Young Prince Rakoto
learns to cope with his father's death.
ISBN 0-8037-1460-2 (trade). — ISBN 0-8037-1461-0 (library)
[1. Folklore — Madagascar.] I. Lewis, E. B., ill. II. Title.
PZ8.1.R2245Ne 1995 398.21 — dc20 [E] 93-28561 CIP AC

The full-color artwork was prepared using
watercolors. It was then scanner-separated and
reproduced as red, blue, yellow, and black halftones.

The author and illustrator thank
Thomas Miller, whose meticulous research helped clarify
crucial details for the illustrations.

Memorial sculptures made of wood (shown opposite)
are found in a variety of styles throughout Madagascar.

· Author's Note ·

The story that the Wise Woman tells Rakoto about the moon and the banana tree is a well-known Malagasy tale. I used this tale as the centerpiece for creating The New King. *The prince's actions after learning of his father's death to his final acceptance of the death are based upon the stages of grief as presented in the work of Dr. Elisabeth Kübler-Ross.*

For John Kempler's family
D. R.

In memory of Dina Rena Mallory
E. B. L.

The loud boom of the drums frightened Prince Rakoto. He dropped his toy and ran to the door. Two guards stood stiffly in the hall. The Royal Doctor sped by, his white robe fluttering up and down. Rakoto decided to run after him and find out what had happened.

But as he stepped into the corridor, a guard blocked his way. "Your mother wants you to stay here."

Rakoto wanted to disobey, but he knew he could never sneak past the guards. For a while he watched the passing flurry of feet and robes. Then he played with his toy again and forgot the commotion outside.

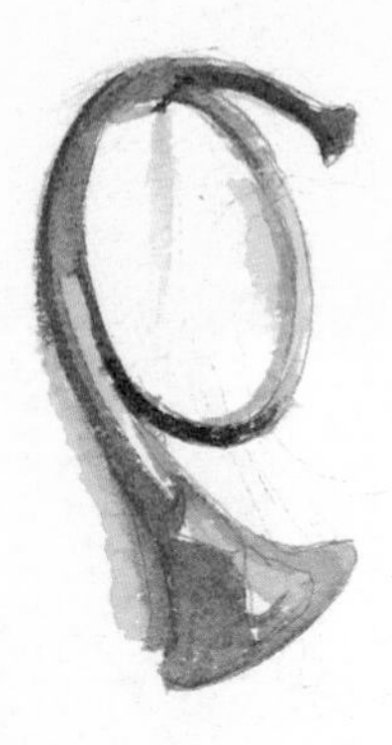

A few hours later his mother walked into his room.

But where was Father? No matter how busy his father was, he always came to take Rakoto to lunch.

Rakoto's mother sat down next to him. Her eyes were red, as if she had rubbed them too hard. "Rakoto." Her usually strong voice trembled.

"Where's Father?" Rakoto asked.

"He's gone."

"Where?"

His mother's chest heaved. "Father won't be with us today... or any other day." She took his small hands in hers. Her hands felt cold. "He was killed during a hunt. There was no way to save his life."

Rakoto stared at his mother.

"I know it's hard to believe," she said, "but Father is dead. Now you are king."

She stretched her arms out to encircle him.

But Rakoto did not want to be held. He slipped out of her arms and ran out of the room.

"Father! Father!" he screamed, racing to his father's chamber.

Four women flanked the doorway. He peered into the room. His father was lying in the middle of a huge stone. He ran across the floor.

"Father!" He climbed up on the stone and pulled his father's hand. But his father did not answer. He pulled again. "Father!" He pulled harder and harder. Then he banged his father's hand with his fist over and over again until he collapsed sobbing.

His mother had been watching from the doorway. She came to him and took him in her arms. "I know how much it hurts," she whispered. She rocked him back and forth. He closed his eyes and surrendered to her soothing embrace.

When he awakened, Rakoto was back in his room and his mother was sleeping at his side. Cautiously he inched away from her and tiptoed out of the room.

Then he ran. Down the hall, out of the palace, to the Royal Doctor's house.

Without announcing himself, he pushed open the front door and shouted, "Sir, are you the greatest doctor this kingdom has ever known?"

The doctor strutted back and forth. "Well, your majesty, I have heard others say so."

"I have heard too. So in my first act as king, I am rewarding you for your skill...if you use your knowledge to bring my father back to life."

The doctor stiffened. He rubbed his knuckles over his bottom lip and stared into the distance. Then he spoke softly. "Your majesty, I cannot do that, even if you command me. Doctors cannot bring people back to life. Doctors cannot perform miracles."

"Then what good is your medicine?" Rakoto snapped and ran out the door to find the Royal Magician.

"Imperial Wizard," he shouted as he pushed open the door, "are you the greatest magician this kingdom has ever known?"

The magician swept his arms up into the air and cuckoos appeared. "I have heard others say so."

"To prove how great you are, I command you to bring my father back to life."

The birds swooped down and pecked at the magician's head. He flicked his hands and they disappeared. Then he said softly, "Your majesty, I cannot do that, even if you command me. Life and death are not matters of magic."

"Then what good is your magic?" Rakoto growled and ran out the door, twisting and turning through the prickly-pear bushes, to see the High Councilor.

"High Councilor," he bellowed, "are you the wisest judge this kingdom has ever known?"

The councilor folded his arms and nodded. "I have heard others say so."

"Then I order you to find the perfect punishment for the Royal Doctor and the Imperial Wizard."

"What are their crimes?" the High Councilor asked.

"I commanded them to bring my father back to life. They will not do it!"

The High Councilor's arms fell to his sides. Then he said softly, "Your majesty, they cannot do that, even if you command them. Doctors do not perform miracles. Magicians do not have the power to turn death into life."

Rakoto opened his mouth as if to speak, but he didn't. Instead he ran to the Wise Woman.

"Wise Woman," he pleaded, "I do not know what to do. I have commanded the Royal Doctor and Royal Magician to bring my father back to life. They refused. I commanded the High Councilor to punish them. He refused. He told me what I want cannot be done by anyone."

"He is right," she said softly. "We cannot bring your father back to life."

"But why did he die?" Rakoto pleaded. "Is it something I have done?"

"No, your majesty. You have done nothing wrong. Everyone dies. It is part of life. Some people die young. Some die old. It was all decided a long time ago."

She leaned back. Rakoto waited for her to speak again.

"A long time ago," she said, "when the earth was very new, God told the first human couple, 'One day you must die. When it is your turn, do you want to die like the moon or like a banana tree?'

"The couple thought to themselves, what a silly idea.

"'How does one die like the moon?' the woman asked.

"God answered, 'Every month the moon starts out as a sliver.

Each night, little by little, it grows bigger and bigger, until we see its entire face in the sky. Then it gets smaller and smaller, until one night there is no moon. But little by little the moon starts to grow again until it is full.'

"How wonderful, the man thought. If we choose to die like the moon, we will come back to life too.

"'And how does one die like a banana tree?' the woman asked.

"God answered, 'The banana tree grows and sends forth shoots. One day the tree dies. But the shoots keep growing until they are big enough and strong enough to send out their own shoots.'

"'I want to die like the moon and live forever,' said the man.

"'But the moon has no one to care for and no one to care for it,' the woman said. 'I do not want to live that way. I want to live like the banana tree. I want us to send forth shoots. I want children.'

"'But then we will die and never return,' the man argued.

"'But while we live, we will love each other and our children. And when we die, our children will carry on our work.'

"'But is that worth the chance to live forever?' the man asked.

"'Giving life to others is a way of living forever,' the woman answered.

"The man thought about what the woman said, and agreed. And since that day each person spends only one lifetime on earth."

The Wise Woman paused. "Your majesty, your father gave you the gift of life. While he lived, he passed on what he knew. These things are part of you now.

"They will always be part of you. And so will your father, even though he is no longer by your side."

Tears rolled down Rakoto's face.

"Can you understand that, my son?" Rakoto turned and saw his mother. He nodded his head up and down, took her hand, and they walked slowly out of the room.

Rakoto took his place as ruler of his people. The years passed and the boy became a man. He ruled with love and justice as his father had taught him, and he passed his father's lessons on to his children.